Yul
Rich

Satan and the Sinneress

No Place in Hell for Angels

Yul Rich

FSC
www.fsc.org
MIX
Papier aus ver-
antwortungsvollen
Quellen
Paper from
responsible sources
FSC® C105338

Imprint

Title:
Satan and the Sinneress

Subtitle:
No Place in Hell for Angels

Author:
© 2024 Yul Rich

Yul.Rich@online.de

Verlag:
BoD · Books on Demand GmbH,
In de Tarpen 42, 22848 Norderstedt
Druck:
Libri Plureos GmbH, Friedensallee 273,
22763 Hamburg
ISBN:
978-3-7693-0651-4

Index

Picture-Credits

The images on the book cover as well as the illustrations in the book were generated by AI and modified with photo manipulation programs.

English edition

This story was originally written in German and then translated into English using artificial intelligence. The AI translation was revised and corrected at some points. If you have any suggestions for improvement, please send an e-mail to: Yul.Rich@online.de

Christa and her bathhouse

Christa was a woman blessed with a beauty that took the breath away of anyone who saw her.

The men did everything to please her and be in her favor.

Christa flirted with all the men and let the men finance a luxurious life for her.

There was no man who did not hope to take Christa as his wife, but she married none.

Secretly, Christa thought to herself:

"Why should I marry a rich man when I can take money from all the rich men in the world?"

There was one man who particularly liked this devilish mindset, and that was Satan, the devil himself.

Realizing that men invested a lot of money to enjoy company of a beautiful woman, Christa opened a bathhouse and hired escort ladies.

Her wellness club was a brothel in disguise. For a high entrance fee, the club offered wellness services such as massages, the use of solarium, sauna, whirlpool, VIP rooms and adult entertainment.

Christa was the boss of the bathhouse and had receptionists collect the entrance fees at the door and lock them in a safe.

She herself watched what was going on in her club while sitting on a golden throne like a queen. To complete the image of her as a goddess, she had air fanned to her from left and right, by servants who looked like slaves and wore only a loincloth.

In addition, maids knelt before her, handing her grapes and other morsels of pleasure.

Apart from the modern hairstyle she wore, she behaved and looked like the reincarnation of Queen Cleopatra at the court of the Emperor of Rome..

Christa left the flirting of the male visitors to other beautiful women who also possessed the art of capitalizing on her beauty.

Immediately after entering the wellness club, the visitors were led by the ladies first to the changing rooms and then to the shower rooms.

There, the men were first soaped by the beautiful ladies. Later, during their stay in the establishment, they were cunningly ensnared and pampered.

The hanky-panky usually resulted in the men losing their minds and promising the ladies gifts of money in exchange for joining them in an undisturbed togetherness, where they would be granted a release from the tensions of the day.

Christa personally hosted only very rich VIP guests in her club, i.e. owners of listed public companies who were at least billionaires.

In the case of mutual sympathy, some of these men were allowed to invite Christa on a cruise on the billionaire's private yacht. Christa usually accepted the invitation if the duration of the trip was limited to a maximum of 2 weeks and if she also received a monetary gift of $2 million per week of travel.

The news of Christa's bathhouse was also heard by Satan, the devil.

One day, it was the 31st day of October, Satan took the form of a man and set out to take Christa's soul.

At the reception of the bathhouse Satan was asked to pay the entrance fee and then follow the assistants to the shower and the changing rooms.

But Satan said:

"I am not an ordinary guest. I would like to speak to Christa, the boss."

Eve, the receptionist replied:

"That's what many visitors say. Who are you and in what matter would you like to speak to Christa?"

"My name is Satan, I am also called the devil. I am the ruler of the underworld and I want to talk to the club owner about her soul."

Eve contorted her face in disbelief, then picked up the phone. While looking fearlessly into Satan's eyes, she spoke:

"Christa, there's a man here at the front desk who doesn't want to pay admission. He claims to be the devil and he said he wants to take your soul or something like that."

Christa's laughter and her voice rang out from the phone:

"It sounds like the man has imagination. I would like to get to know him. I want him to take a shower like all men. After half an hour, Angela may bring him to me."

Eve repeated what Christa had said and added:

"You actually have a date with Christa. Now, shoo, shoo, get into the shower."

Devil or not?

Eve signaled Angela, who in turn waved to two other assistants.

Anna and Cathy hooked up with Satan left and right and accompanied him to the locker rooms. There they took off his clothes and hung them carefully in a locker.

When Satan took off his shoes and stockings, the shower assistants discovered that this guest had a misshapen foot that looked like a horse's foot.

Cathy said to Satan:

"Anna is going to soap you up in the shower now, I have to go back to the front desk, I'll be right back and join both of you."

While Anna entered the shower rooms with Satan, Cathy rushed to the reception and alerted Angela and Eve:

"The guy who claims he is Satan actually has a horse's foot, like the devil. He also has dark red strangely hairy skin, but it's not red from sunburn. I don't know what to make of that, but just to be on the safe side, I'll tell you: he really does look like what you'd imagine the devil to look like."

Eve replied:

"Thank you, Cathy, we will inform Christa. Now go back to Satan and glamour him like we glamour all men."

Cathy nodded and went back to the devil, straight into the shower rooms, where Anna was in the process of soaping up the devil's thing.

To Cathy's shock, however, the thing was not of the kind that the shower ladies usually soap up, but a completely different body part: it grew out of Satan's extended spine.

16

Eve stood at the reception desk and looked at Angela.

"What do you think? Should we tell Christa what Cathy saw? Surely he's not a devil. I guess, he has just a crippled club foot."

"You better call her," Angela said.

Eve nodded, called Christa and told her what Cathy had seen in the locker room.

Christa replied:

"Okay, we'll arrange a test. We do have a prop room with angel costumes for the Halloween parties. Have Angela bring me one right away. I'll send out four more ladies, have them dress in angel costumes, hang crucifixes around their necks, and head to the blue Paradise Room. The shower ladies must keep him busy for at least half an hour, then lead him to the Paradise Room. Understood?"

"Ay, ay, Christa. Got it," Eve said and immediately let Angela in on the plan.

Christa sat on her throne and ordered her two servants to immediately recruit a total of four ladies who right now did not have a master to pamper.

Three minutes later the servants and four beauties stood before Christa's throne and Christa spoke:

"Girls, I ask for your attention and that you help me with a little role play."

The ladies nodded and listened to what Christa would say:

"We have a VIP guest; he plays the devil and you should all be angels. I ask you to play along, I'm in too. Please go to the prop room now, dress up as innocent pretty angels. Grab crucifixes, rosaries, holy water and all similar accessories for a heavenly role play in the blue paradise room. Meet me there in exactly 15 minutes, okay?"

"Okay," the ladies shouted and rushed to the wardrobe, where the costumes for the parties and role-playing games were kept.

In the prop room were numerous angel and devil costumes because these were often needed for special events like Halloween and costume parties.

Angela was already there and had picked out a costume for Christa. When the ladies entered the room, she said:

"Our VIP guest is the devil incarnate, so you know! So only wear angel costumes! We'll see you in the blue paradise room in a minute!"

One of the ladies raised her hand and said:

"Sorry, I don't think I can play this game. I am Aga from Poland, and I am strictly Catholic. I am very afraid of the devil, because I really believe that there is God and the devil."

Angela, however, replied:

"Very good, Aga. Then you know that God's love can always defeat the devil. God is by your side in this game precisely because you believe in Him. This is true for all of you: the more you believe in God, the better it is for this game! It is a matter of driving the devil out of this man we are about to meet! Now, everyone, hallelujah!"

"Hallelujah!" the ladies shouted.

After showering, Satan was handed a white bathrobe by Anna, but he refused it and asked for a black or red one.

"We don't have black robes, but we do have red towels. Would that be okay?"

Satan said yes and Cathy quickly got two large bath towels in red color.

"Why two?" asked Satan

"One towel to dry off and the second big bath towel to use as a loincloth so you don't walk around the club completely naked," said Cathy, who was wearing only a tiny white bikini.

The devil casually laid the towel over his shoulder while Anna tied Satan's bath towel around his waist and knotted it skillfully so that it wouldn't slip down again immediately.

Then the bikini-girls Anna and Cathy set off with the VIP guest to show him the wellness club and its facilities during a tour: sauna, whirlpool, etc..

The tour usually lasted a few minutes, but Anna and Cathy had to buy time so that Christa and the angel-ladies could prepare for the meeting with the devil.

So, Satan was asked at each wellness-station to give it a quick try. He received a short massage, had to briefly enter the sauna, get into the whirlpool, briefly take a seat in the cinema room and taste a bite from the buffet in the club's restaurant.

Satan liked the way the ladies showed him around, but at some point, he asked impatiently:

"When do I get to talk to the boss?"

Cathy looked at her wristwatch for a moment and said, "I think the thirty minutes are up, and Christa has time for you now. I hope so."

Satan was now escorted to the throne where Christa usually always sat.

But she was not there.

Paradise Room

"Where is Christa?" Cathy asked the servant standing next to the throne.

"Please follow me," said the servant and went ahead.

In front of the blue paradise room, the servant stopped and said to Satan:

"Christa is waiting for you in this room. Cathy, Anna, ladies first, you two go ahead."

After saying this, the servant stood behind Satan.

The two ladies of the house stepped in front of Satan, opened the door, and entered the room.

The servant pushed the devil into the room and immediately shut the door behind him.

Anna and Cathy stepped to the side and the devil was very frightened when he saw in what kind of room he was and what kind of ladies were waiting for him here.

The devil was standing in the Paradise Room, which not only looked heavenly, but was also furnished that way: the walls and ceiling were blue, and in the middle was a four-poster bed covered with blue bedding.

The four bedposts rose to the ceiling and attached to them was a canopy from which hung fabric linens, they were above the bed and also fell behind the bed and down the sides to the floor.

At the head of the bed sat Christina, dressed in a white robe, like an angel. Above her head hovered a golden halo discreetly fastened in her hair.

Two more ladies dressed in angel costumes sat on the bed to the left and right of Christa, and two angel ladies also stood at the left and right bedposts.

Christa looked like a goddess, surrounded by angels and said:

"Dear angels, greet my guest with a triple 'Hallelujah!'"

And the angels sang in chorus:

"Hallelujah! Hallelujah! Hallelujah!"

This hurt the devil and he covered his ears with his hands.

After the hallelujah shouts had died down, Christa asked the devil:

"I was told that you are the devil, that your name is Satan, and you want to talk with me. How do you like the reception we have organized for you?"

"I don't like it at all, because I'm really the devil," said Satan.

"You can't have a good role-play without angels, though, don't you think?" asked Christa with a smile, and the angels shouted a "Hallelujah!" in confirmation.

"I didn't come to do a role-playing game. I came to get your soul," said the devil.

"You don't really think that my soul will leave this beautiful paradise room with you? Please enjoy your stay in my establishment. When will you have the opportunity to be in heaven surrounded by angels?"

The devil replied:

"I see I can't reason with you as long as you sit like a goddess on this heavenly bed and are guarded by your angels. I'll come back another time. Someday I will get you and then you will go to hell together with me!"

Satan turned to leave the Paradise Room, but he could not open the door because: There was a large crucifix hanging on the door and the two angels who had been standing at the bedpost before were now guarding the door.

He turned to Christa again and was about to say something, but she beat him to it:

"No guest of my house leaves the club without donating an appropriately valuable gift for the ladies. And since you had a rendez-vous with me, the boss, the gift must be exceptionally valuable."

Satan was irritated.

"What precious thing shall I give you, Mrs. Chr...", said the devil, and Christa's name stuck in his throat, for he could not pronounce it.

He continued:

"You collect several million every time from the lords you meet, and you have all the worldly riches one could wish for. However, you cannot take these riches with you when you pass away. Neither in heaven nor in hell will all your money be of any use to you. You do not need a gift from me! Now release the door so that I can leave again!"

Christa laughed.

"Thank you for telling me that I can't take the riches with me after I die. But you cannot leave my club without giving me a valuable gift. Therefore, I suggest you promise me that you will never again be interested in my soul, and never again come to take my soul or those of the ladies here. If you promise this, we will remove the crucifix from the door and allow you to leave our club again."

The devil looked aghast into Christa's eyes and then into the faces of the angels present. He looked at the door again, but the sight of the crucifix hurt his eyes.

He looked again at Christa and her angels, and he almost felt dizzy because he was aware that he was locked in the Paradise Room.

Christa noticed that the devil was weakened and started shouting "Hallelujah!" and all the angels in the room joined in and sang along.

The devil raised his hand and shouted:

"Okay, so be it! You may keep your souls forever; I have no interest in you! Now stop singing and let me go!"

Christa and the angel ladies stopped singing and Christa asked:

"Did I understand that correctly? Please repeat again."

The devil nodded and confirmed:

"You have understood correctly. All of you who are here in the room may keep your soul, will never go to hell. I never want to see you again!"

All ladies shouted "Hallelujah", and the devil covered his ears again.

Cathy removed the crucifix from the door and opened it.

The devil turned around once more and looked Christa hatefully in the eyes. Christa, however, only grinned and waved her hand gracefully in farewell.

Cathy and Anna accompanied the devil to the changing room, took the towels from him and threw them into the bag for used laundry.

Then they walked with Satan to the exit, where Eve asked them, "Does Mr. Satan have to pay anything else?"

Cathy and Anna answered in the negative.

Eve asked Satan:

"Was everything to your liking? Were you satisfied with the service of our ladies?"

The devil stamped his horse's foot and left the bathhouse growling and cursing.

After Years

Christa and her ladies lived happily ever after, enjoying their lives, and becoming richer and richer.

One day a very rich multi-billionaire came and invited Christa and all the ladies to have a boat party on his private yacht.

While they were sailing on the high seas, the big yacht suddenly exploded for some unknown reason. The ship caught fire, sank, and all the people drowned and died.

Suddenly, Christa, her ladies, and the billionaire were standing in front of Saint Peter at the pearly gates of heaven.

Peter checked the guest list, but only the billionaire was allowed into heaven.

Christa asked:

"Why is it that the rich guy is allowed to come in and we women are not?"

Peter stated:

"The rich man was a believer in God and throughout his life, he always donated a lot of money to the church and numerous other charitable organizations. Therefore, he is allowed to pass the pearly gate to heaven.

But you, Christa, and you ladies, you shamelessly exploited the men's need for affection and spent the money you collected only on expensive cars, luxury goods, jewelry, shoes, handbags, and clothes. You never donated anything for the poor. You will be punished for your selfishness and will not be allowed to enter heaven. I will call a cab to pick you up and you will go to hell."

Christa complained and the ladies started to whine, but Peter wouldn't budge.

The Hell Cab arrived, a small bus. At the wheel was none other than Beelzebub, the second highest prince of hell after Satan, the devil.

"Get in the car," Beelzebub ordered, then he and the ladies went to hell.

Arriving at the entrance to hell, Christa and her friends suddenly found themselves in front of Satan himself.

Christa recognized him immediately and complained:

"Hello Satan, do you recognize us? You promised us back in the bathhouse that you didn't want our soul and we wouldn't have to go to hell."

Satan frowned, looked twice at the ladies' faces, then said:

"I remember. I have no interest in your souls, and you do not have to go to hell as I promised. Beelzebub, take the ladies back to heaven and tell Peter that we will not admit the ladies to hell."

Christa and the ladies got back into the Hell Cab and Beelzebub drove back to the Gates of Heaven.

"Hello Peter, nice greeting from Satan, the ladies don't have to go to hell. Because we don't let them in, I brought them back."

The ladies got out of the cab and Beelzebub left the ladies in front of the heaven's gate and drove away.

"I need to talk to the boss," Peter said, called God, explained the situation, and learned that he was not allowed to let the ladies into heaven.

"What?" cried Christa. "Neither heaven nor hell is meant for us? What the hell are we supposed to do now!"

Peter passed the question on to God:

"What are the damned women supposed to do now? If we don't let them go to heaven, and the devil doesn't let them go to hell, they will have to wander around in limbo for eternity."

"So be it!" said God, and continued, "Give the ladies a plain simple ghost robe and a candle, so that they can see and can be seen on their dark paths between heaven and hell. To be of some use, they are supposed to scare people as ghosts and remind them that one must always live well-behaved in order to go to heaven."

Peter handed out white cloaks to the ladies, which looked like burkas: they covered the whole body and also the face. So that they could see through with their eyes, the ghostly garment had two holes.

He also gave the ladies candles that would never go out and would burn for eternity.

Finally, Peter gave them some advice:

"You have the best effect on people when you ghost around for an hour after midnight, that's why that time is called the witching hour.

Every year, on October 31, you will meet people who also dress up like ghosts. Some, instead of a candle, carry a pumpkin with a grimace carved into it and a candle inside.

This is in memory of 'Jack with the lantern', a blacksmith who, like you, has gone neither to heaven nor to hell. He has received an eternally glowing coal from Satan, which he carries in a pumpkin like a lantern, just like you carry the candles.

Now have fun ghosting!"

End

Aga

The story is almost told, and sympathetic readers may wonder if the strictly Catholic Polish woman named Aga was not let into heaven either.

For consolation, it can be added that Aga was very lucky.

Shortly after Satan's visit to the bathhouse, Aga decided to quit her job as a hostess.

When a rich man visited the spa club and fell in love with Aga, he asked her to marry him. Aga took the chance, said 'yes' and became the man's wife. From then on, she no longer worked at Christa's club, but only pampered her husband.

Consequently, she was not on the yacht when it sank, and all the 'sinners' suddenly stood before Peter and did not go to heaven.

Aga and her millionaire lived happily ever after, and both went to heaven.

Final End

Afterword

The idea for the story came about when the author, searching on the Internet for legends from Ireland, accidentally discovered the story "Jack o' Lantern".

The "Legend of Jack with the Lantern", tells about "Stingy Jack", who was neither admitted to heaven nor to hell and has to walk as a ghost in nowhere until eternity. The Legend is told in many variations and is now understood as an explanation why people hollow out pumpkins on Halloween, cut grimaces into them and light them up from the inside.

Yul Rich imagined how the ancient Irish legend could be transposed to modern times and what it would be like if the devil were tricked by a woman. Finally, the author created the present adaptation: "Satan and the Sinneress".

So that readers don't have to go to the trouble of now searching the Internet for the story of Jack and the Devil, the following pages feature the legend of "Jack and the Lantern" as retold by the author in the pub when he wants to draw attention to this book.

The Halloween-Legend

The Irish Legend of Jack with the Lantern

Retelling by Yul Rich:

From Ireland originate many old legends, yes, the Irish have a hell of a lot of crazy imagination. They invented mermaids who can only live in the sea because they wear a magic cap, and they invented the story of Jack with the lantern. That's the reason you always see those glowing pumpkins at Halloween.

The legend of Jack goes like this:

It's been a long time, it was sometime in the Middle Ages or even earlier, but there were already taverns and blacksmiths. Jack was such a blacksmith, but he was also a stingy scoundrel, a sly one who wasn't exactly honest, and he also liked to go to pubs to drink.

One evening, it was October 31st, when Jack was sitting at the bar once again and drinking, the devil came to take his soul.

The devil sat down next to Jack on the bar stool and said:

"You're due now, come with me to hell."

Jack wanted to argue, but the devil wouldn't listen. Then Jack said:

"But before I go with you, I think I have one last wish."

"What's that?"

"You have to buy me one last beer."

The devil agreed and ordered another beer for Jack. Unfortunately, the devil had no money with him. To be able to pay, he turned himself into a coin.

Don't ask me why the devil had to turn into a coin, but he did, or the legend wouldn't go on.

So, Jack suddenly saw the coin lying on the counter, but instead of paying for the beer with it, he swiped the coin and put it in his pocket.

Because Jack also had a key chain with a crucifix in it in his pocket, the devil, meaning the coin, was now right next to the crucifix, and the devil was trapped in the pocket and could do nothing but whine.

"Get me out of here," the devil pleaded, but Jack said:

"Bite me! You stay in there. If I let you out, you'll get my soul and I'll go to hell. No, no, I won't let you out of there."

The devil, however, wanted to be free again and eventually made a pact with Jack: If Jack would release him again, the devil would leave him alone for ten years.

That was okay with Jack, so he gave the devil his freedom again and the devil left.

After ten years, however, the devil came back and said:

"Hi Jack, the ten years are up, now I'm coming for you."

Jack nodded, but he insisted on getting one more last meal. The devil had to grant him his last wish, of course.

Well, I would have ordered a juicy steak, but Jack wanted an apple from the apple tree that was in front of the pub.

The two went to the apple tree and the devil climbed the tree to pick an apple.

Cunning Jack quickly pulled out his knife and carved a cross into the bark of the apple tree and: Fact, the devil could no longer get down from the tree because the holy cross was in his way.

The devil now sat on the tree and could not get down and moaned:

"Hey Jack, I can't stay in the tree forever, now please remove the cross!"

Jack let the devil whine around and finally the devil was ready to promise Jack that he would never ever bother him again.

In other words, Jack would never have to go to hell if he let the devil down from the tree.

Jack then used his knife to scrape the cross off the bark of the tree and the devil was free again, cursing about not being able to get Jack's soul.

Jack laughed to himself and lived his scoundrel life for many more years.

At some point, Jack died and stood before the gates of heaven, wanting to get in.

But St. Peter said:

"No, Jack, you're a scoundrel, you've ripped off and fooled everyone in your life, you can't get in here."

Thus, Jack was not allowed into heaven, and St. Peter scolded him to the devil.

Jack then went to the gates of hell and there stood Satan in front of him and said:

"Hello Jack, what are you doing here? You're not going to hell, that was the deal."

The Jack was all confused and didn't know where to go. He was not allowed to go anywhere, neither to heaven nor to hell.

"Where am I supposed to go now?" asked Jack, and the devil said:

"You'll have to ghost around in nowhere now. Here, take this, here's a light so you can see something in the dark."

The devil gave Jack a piece of glowing burning coal, straight from the hellfire.

Jack had a large turnip with him, on which he put the coal and thus had something like a torch to light his way.

That was the story of dishonest, deceitful Jack.

Parents always told it to the children as a warning that one should always be good. So that you would go to heaven and not to hell or wander around as a ghost.

Every year, on October 31, the children play "Jack with the lantern". For the sake of simplicity, the torch with the turnip and the coal was transformed into a hollowed-out pumpkin with a candle inside. So, now it's clear why you can see these glowing pumpkins everywhere on Halloween. And to make it look a little creepier, they carve grimaces into the pumpkins.

Another version of the original story can be found at:

https://www.history.com/news/history-of-the-jack-o-lantern-irish-origins

Wikipedia publishes even more information and reveals other versions of "Jack with the lantern" or "Jack-o'-Lantern".

The strange link has an apostrophe:

https://en.wikipedia.org/wiki/Jack-o'-lantern

Afterword II

The ladies of the bathhouse are modeled on the service ladies of the so-called FKK Sauna Clubs that are widespread in Germany. In the end, however, the author has the sinneresses wander around not with a jack-o'-lantern like Jack, but as ghosts with a candle. In the process, the author asked himself why ghosts are actually so often depicted with a candle, and passed the question on to the AI.

In the author's opinion, you.com provided the best answer to the question, "Why do ghosts always carry a candle?"

Symbolic representation of life after death: one interpretation is that the candle represents the light of the spirit or soul. It symbolizes the transition between life and death and lights the way for the departed soul in the afterlife. The candle can be seen as an orientation light that helps the spirit to find its way in the darkness or to find the way to the afterlife.

Puns

created by Yul Rich after having written the story
"Satan and the Sinneress":

It is not enough to identify yourself as an angel.
You must be a real one.

No Place in Hell for Angels.

The place of honor in hell
is for proud sinners only.

Sinners go to hell. Angels go to heaven.
Fakers go nowhere.

Hell is only for sinners who have no regrets.

ALWAYS BE AN ANGEL.
IF YOU CAN'T BE AN ANGEL,
BE A REAL DEVIL.

Be an Insider or an Outsider.
Don't stay in the Limbo.

About the author

Yul Rich is the pen name of a German author and self-publisher who loves to come up with fantasy and love stories. His ideas are inspired by kissing muses and everyday life, but also by ancient sagas and legends.
Lately, he has even drawn inspiration from artificial intelligence.

Whatever he writes, Yul Rich wants his stories to touch the reader's heart.

yul.rich@online.de